Sam's Spots

First published in 2008 by
Franklin Watts
338 Euston Road
London
NW1 3BH

Franklin Watts Australia
Level 17/207 Kent Street
Sydney
NSW 2000

A CIP catalogue record for this book is available
from the British Library.

ISBN 978 0 7496 7976 7 (hbk)
ISBN 978 0 7496 7984 2 (pbk)

Series Editor: Jackie Hamley
Series Advisor: Dr Barrie Wade
Series Designer: Peter Scoulding

Printed in China

Franklin Watts is a division of
Hachette Children's Books,
an Hachette Livre UK company.

To Lia, with love – C.J.

Sam's Spots

by Caryn Jenner

Illustrated by Jonathan Langley

W
FRANKLIN WATTS
LONDON • SYDNEY

Sam was excited about his birthday.

He had invited lots of
friends to his party.

But there was a problem.

Sam felt itchy all over.

"You're very spotty,"
said Dad the next day.

"You've got chicken pox,"
said Mum.

"We can't have your party until you're better," said Dad.

Sam was upset.

Mum gave Sam a bath
with special oil in it.

Dad covered Sam's spots
with special lotion.

His sister, Lily, tried
to cheer him up.

"Birthdays are full of surprises!" she said.

"Even spotty birthdays?"
Sam grumbled.

"Wait and see,"
smiled Lily.

On his birthday, Sam woke up feeling sad. Then Lily came into his bedroom.

She had painted spots
all over her face.
Sam laughed.

Happy
birthday,
Sam!

He laughed at Mum
and Dad, too.

"Now we're all spotty,"
said Mum.

There were lots of spotty surprises.

They all played pin the
spots on the donkey ...

... and pass the spotty parcel.

Then they ate spotty
birthday cake.

"There's one more spotty surprise," Lily told Sam.

"Something you've always wanted."

"Spotty birthdays are the best! I'm going to call him Spot!" laughed Sam.

Leapfrog has been specially designed to fit the requirements of the National Literacy Framework. It offers real books for beginning readers by top authors and illustrators. There are 26 Leapfrog stories to choose from:

Rhyming stories
are available with
Leapfrog Rhyme Time.

* hardback